CUMBRIA LIBRARIES

3 8003 04843 1571

KT-491-434

for Jonathan

and in loving memory of Porridge,
who wouldn't get her paws off my drawings
F.S.

First published in 2017 by Scholastic Children's Books
Euston House, 24 Eversholt Street, London NW1 1DB
a division of Scholastic Ltd

www.scholastic.co.uk

London ~ New York ~ Toronto ~ Sydney ~ Auckland
Mexico City ~ New Delhi ~ Hong Kong

Text and illustrations copyright © 2017 Fabi Santiago

Edited by Pauliina Malinen
Designed by Strawberrie Donnelly

ISBN: 978 1407 17148 7

All rights reserved • Printed in Malaysia

1 3 5 7 9 10 8 6 4 2

The moral rights of Fabi Santiago have been asserted.

Papers used by Scholastic Children's Books
are made from wood grown in
sustainable forests.

FABI SANTIAGO

PAWS OFF MY BOOK

SCHOLASTIC

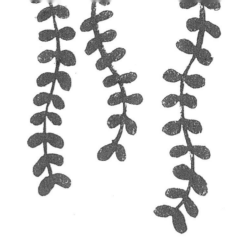

just LOVE reading.

Well hello, **hello**, Olaf!
I haven't seen you in ages.
Not since breakfast!

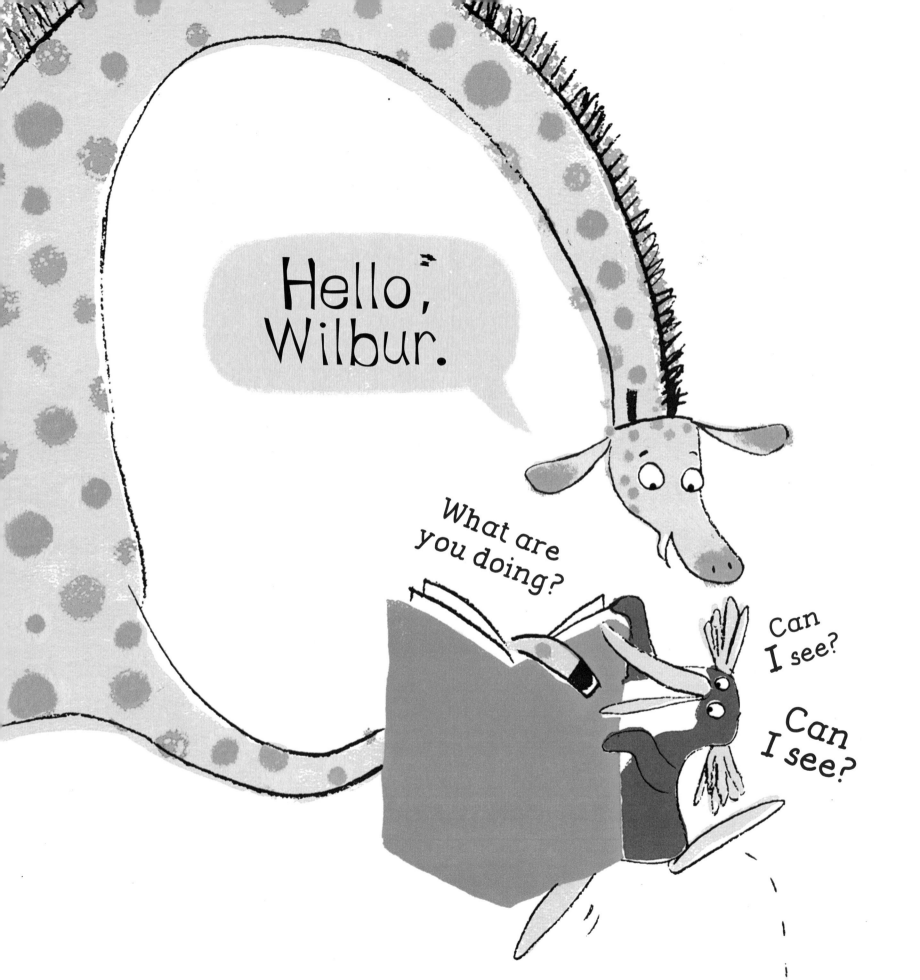

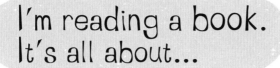
I'm reading a book. It's all about...

Duh!

Ha! You ARE funny! THAT'S not how you read.

Are you sure?

THIS is how you read. See, it's comfy to **sit** on your bottom.

Squidgety Squidgety

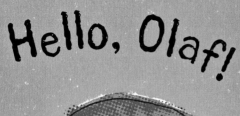

Hello, Olaf!

What are you doing?

Tell me!

Tell me!

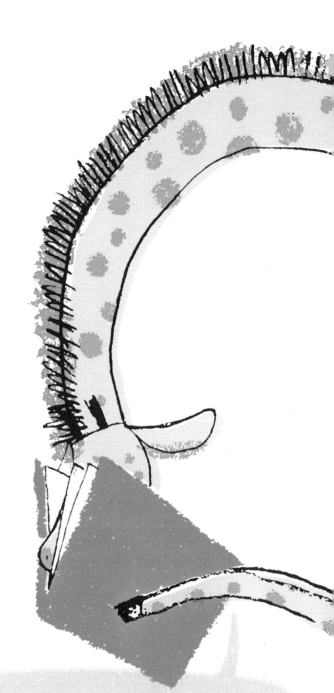

Hi, Matilda!
I'm reading a book. I've just
got to the bit where...

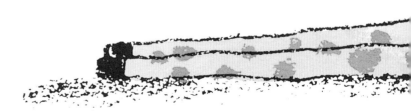

What did you just say?